PUFFI

THE RAILWAY CAT AND DIGBY

Somehow, Alfie the railway cat always seems to be in Leading Railman Hack's bad books. Alfie is a smart cat, a lot smarter than many people think, and he would like to be friends with Hack. But when he tries to improve matters by 'helping' Hack's dog, Digby, win a prize at the local show, things rapidly go from bad to worse!

Between them, Alfie and Digby have some hilarious adventures – but clearly they are going to have to do something amazing to change Hack's mind about Alfie!

Phyllis Arkle was born and educated in Chester, but now lives in the Thames Valley village of Twyford, Berkshire. In addition to reading and writing, she is actively interested in the Women's Institute movement.

The Railway Cat and Digby

PHYLLIS ARKLE

Illustrated by Lynne Byrnes

PUFFIN BOOKS

Puffin Books, Penguin Books Ltd, Harmondsworth, Middlesex, England
Viking Penguin Inc., 40 West 23rd Street, New York, New York 10010, U.S.A.
Penguin Books Australia Ltd, Ringwood, Victoria, Australia
Penguin Books Canada Limited, 2801 John Street, Markham, Ontario, Canada L3R 1B4
Penguin Books (N.Z.) Ltd, 182–190 Wairau Road, Auckland 10, New Zealand

First published by Hodder & Stoughton Children's Books 1984
Published in Puffin Books 1986
Reprinted 1986

Copyright © Phyllis Arkle, 1984
Illustrations copyright © Hodder & Stoughton Ltd, 1984
All rights reserved

Made and printed in Great Britain by Cox & Wyman Ltd, Reading

Contents

1

Station Visitors

A pale early morning sun shone through the waiting room window. In his basket Alfie, the railway cat, stretched himself happily. Winter was nearly over. Spring days were ahead and there was plenty of activity at the station.

Today, for instance, Alfie's great friend Fred, the Chargeman, was going to show a group of school children round the station – and who better than Alfie to lead the way?

The railway cat left his basket and leapt through a partly-open ventilator on to the platform. He made his way over the bridge and sat down outside the staff room door. Leading Railman Hack, who lived just up the road from the station, would be reporting for duty soon.

Not that Alfie especially wanted to see Hack, who was often grumpy, and didn't like cats – Alfie was ready for breakfast. He never minded seeing

Hack's dog, Digby. As a matter of fact, although there was always a skirmish – just for fun – whenever the two animals met, Alfie really liked Digby. Alfie also got on well with Hack's pigeons, occasionally chasing them off the station platform for a game.

But – hello, hello – what was this? Alfie blinked. Was he dreaming, or was Hack coming briskly towards him, calling out cheerfully, 'Sorry to keep you waiting, Alfie. I'll get your breakfast in two shakes of a lamb's tail.'

Alfie followed the man into the staff room. Sure enough, in about *ten* shakes of a lamb's tail (according to Alfie's reckoning) Hack placed a saucer of catmeat and another saucer of milk on the floor. Alfie bent his head and set to. Breakfast was breakfast whoever served it.

As he lapped the milk he wondered why Hack was so happy and excited this morning. Then he remembered. Of course – Punch! Hack's racing pigeon Punch, had been entered in a national long-distance race. The bird was expected to return to Hack's garden loft some time this morning, to be timed in. Punch had been tipped favourite to win the race.

Alfie raised his head as Hack spoke. 'Fred's given me permission to go off duty for an hour or so after the rush period. I must be near my pigeon loft to check Punch's arrival time. Very important race this, Alfie.'

'Miaow!' agreed Alfie, as he put his head down again.

When he had finished his meal, Alfie strolled over to the main exit. While he waited for Fred to arrive, he sat down and started to wash himself. He gave his long shiny whiskers and eyebrows special attention.

Fred came along. 'Good morning, Alfie,' he cried. 'Getting ready for the visitors? Shall I brush your whiskers?'

'Prrr-rr . . . Prrr-rr . . . Prrr-rr . . .' sang Alfie as he weaved in and out of Fred's legs.

Brown, the Booking Clerk, came on duty. He eyed the grey and white striped cat admiringly. 'My word, Alfie,' he said. 'You're a credit to the station.'

10

'Miaow!' said Alfie, thinking how jolly everyone was this morning. Long might it last!

Alfie was kept busy for the next two hours, seeing passengers in and out of trains. He always remembered to stand well back from the platform edge when express trains approached. Now and then he ran to the front of the station to see if there was any sign of the children.

'Impatient!' laughed Fred. 'It's not nearly time yet.'

But soon it *was* time and Alfie took up his position to greet the children. His head jerked from side to side and his ears twitched.

Then he heard a murmur of voices and round a corner came a crocodile of children and two teachers. Some of the children were carrying pencils and notebooks, some pencils and drawing pads. They pointed and shouted when they saw Alfie.

'Alfie's there!'

'He's waiting for *us*.'

'He'll show us round the station.'

'I'm sure he's capable of doing that,' laughed one of the teachers.

Hack passed on his way home. 'Have a good time,' he called.

Alfie ran back into the station and miaowed loudly outside the booking office. Brown opened the door. Alfie entered and leapt up on to a wide counter in front of the glass partition. He sat down beside the ticket machine. As the children filed into the hall, they saw Alfie peering at them through the glass circle which had SPEAK HERE underneath. The children surged forward.

'Ticket to Edinburgh, please,' cried one boy.

'Ticket to Newcastle . . .'

'Ticket to Penzance . . .'

'Ticket to Llanfairpwllgwyngyllgogerychwyrn-drobwllllantysiliogogogoch!' shouted a Welsh boy.

'Now then, that's enough,' said a teacher, with a smile. 'We're here to learn how the station is run, not to play games.'

'Alfie evidently thinks you should be shown round the booking office first, so follow me,' said Fred.

Inside Brown said to a boy, 'Order a ticket to anywhere – single, return, weekend, just choose.'

'First class day return ticket to London, please,' said the boy promptly.

Just at that moment Alfie, still on the counter, stretched out a paw and accidentally touched several keys on the ticket machine. Brown then pressed another key and out of the top of the machine emerged a single ticket – to Glasgow!

Everyone laughed and Fred said, 'Stop interfering, Alfie.'

Brown demonstrated the *correct* way to issue a first class day return to London. The children were interested in everything. They made notes, sketched and asked lots of questions.

Next, Alfie led the way to Fred's office. There the timetables were examined, and the teleprinter revealed that one train was running late and another one had been cancelled. Fred glanced at the wall clock. 'Who would like to make an announcement to the passengers?' he asked.

'You, Jim,' said a teacher nodding at a boy.

Fred showed Jim how to operate the Public Address System. The boy pressed the TALK key and spoke into the microphone,

'THE 10.22 TRAIN TO BRISTOL WILL BE ARRIVING SHORTLY AT PLATFORM NO.1.'

Then the boy pressed the Cancel key.

'Very good,' said Fred. 'I'm sure you could be heard all over the station. Now I'll show . . .'

He was interrupted by a cry of, '*I* want a go,' and before anyone realised his intentions, a boy pushed forward, jabbed at the TALK key and yelled.

'FIRE! FI . . .'

As Fred thrust the boy aside, Alfie spied a mouse lurking behind a book on the desk.

Fred started to speak quickly, but calmly, into the microphone, 'CHARGEMAN SPEAKING. THERE IS NO . . .'

Alfie sprang on to the desk and knocked the instrument over. Fred grabbed it. 'GET OFF, ALFIE. *GET OFF*!' he yelled. Then, 'SORRY, PASSENGERS. I REPEAT – THERE IS NO FIRE. NO NEED FOR . . .'

The mouse disappeared. Alfie jumped on to Fred's shoulders and put his front paws on Fred's head, while his eyes searched the room for it.

15

'ALFIE!' shrieked Fred. 'SORRY, PASSEN-GERS. THERE IS NO FIRE. NO NEED FOR PANIC. THE 10.22 TRAIN FOR BRISTOL IS APPROACHING.' Fred was quite breathless.

The mouse scurried down a leg of the desk and, with Alfie in pursuit, dashed on to the platform. Fred followed. All was confusion. The mouse evaded Alfie as it weaved its way between the legs of bewildered passengers. People jumped out of the way as Alfie chased the mouse and Fred tried to catch Alfie.

'Come here, Alfie!' he shouted.

But Alfie turned a deaf ear. The train drew in. By this time Alfie had again lost sight of the mouse but, suddenly, he saw it clinging to a man's trousers. Alfie moved quickly. Too late! Man and mouse had boarded the train. Doors were slammed, a signal given and the train left.

Alfie watched it depart. He hoped the passengers would enjoy having a mouse with them! After all, it wasn't the railway cat's fault if a mouse decided to go on a train journey, was it?

Fred was still breathing heavily as he gazed down

at Alfie. '*Alfie*,' he got out at last. 'I'm surprised at you.' Then he relaxed and grinned. 'It *is* one of your duties to keep the station mouse-free. But watch your step!'

'Miaow!' said Alfie. He was glad Fred understood, and he would be on his best behaviour – for a time at least!

Fred led the way back into the office. The offending boy had been sent home.

'Disgraceful behaviour!' said an embarrassed teacher.

'Well, no real harm has been done,' said Fred. 'Don't let it spoil the morning for the others.'

The children spent another profitable hour at the station. When it was time for them to leave, they thanked Fred and made a fuss of Alfie.

'Can we come again?' they wanted to know.

'Of course,' said Fred.

'Miaow!' added Alfie.

He sat beside Fred on the forecourt and watched the children depart.

'Well, it's back to work for me,' said Fred as he bent down to stroke Alfie.

There was no sign of Hack. Alfie hoped Punch had arrived home, in time to win the race. It had been an exciting but exhausting morning for the railway cat. Time for a nap. The staff room door was open. He went in, curled up in a chair and closed his eyes.

As he dozed off he wondered whether the mouse was enjoying the train journey to Bristol, and if it would be able to find its way back to the station.

2

Punch in the Race

Alfie was in the middle of a beautiful dream about a fish supper, when he was roused by a rustling and fluttering noise on the roof. He opened one eye, twitched an ear and listened. Sleep overcame him – but not for long. The noise began again.

Nuisance, thought Alfie. Must be a bird – a pigeon, perhaps. A *pigeon*! He'd forgotten about Punch and the race. Could it possibly be Punch on the roof? If so, why was the silly bird losing valuable time, when he should be speeding back to Hack's garden loft to be checked in?

Alfie dashed out of the staff room. In one bound he reached the top of the cycle shed and from there had easy access to the flat roof. There he saw a pigeon, dark blue colour above and white underneath, with a rubber ring round one leg. It was undoubtedly Punch.

From his high vantage point, Alfie could see

Hack – and Digby – waiting in the garden. Their heads were raised as they gazed hopefully into the sky for a sight of the homing pigeon. They didn't glance in the station direction, or they might have seen Punch strutting about on the staff room roof. Alfie was amazed that the bird could be so stupid.

Well, here was a wonderful opportunity for Alfie to get into Hack's good books – for a change! He would chase Punch off the roof towards the pigeon loft. How grateful Hack would be when his eyes roved towards the station and saw what Alfie was doing. Fred would be pleased too, when he heard about it.

Alfie crouched low, tensed his muscles – and sprang! Punch flapped his wings in defiance and rose into the air, where he hovered just out of Alfie's reach. With a great effort Alfie leapt higher, but still Punch evaded him. Alfie was baffled. He sat down again. Punch alighted on the far edge of the roof. Warily they gazed at one another.

Fred looked up from the platform. 'Whatever are you doing on the roof, Alfie?' he called. 'Come down at once.'

'Miaow!' said Alfie, without turning his head. Fred must understand that the railway cat was on important business.

On his stomach, Alfie began to sidle up to Punch. Nearer and nearer he got. Suddenly, he jumped and managed to take a couple of gentle swipes at Punch. And to Alfie's relief, the pigeon, making loud cooing noises, flew off – in the right direction.

Punch would win the race. Hack had probably noticed what had happened on the roof and Alfie would get due credit.

But Alfie's joy was short-lived. Punch made a wide circle, and returned to the roof! And each time Alfie chased him off, the bird flew round in circles – and then came back.

Alfie was feeling desperate. Time was passing. At this rate Punch wouldn't have a chance of winning the race. Hack would return to work with a frown on his face. So Alfie pretended to get very angry. He hissed and snarled at Punch, but the pigeon seemed to be *enjoying* himself. He evidently thought it was a very good game.

And at last, it must be admitted, Alfie began to

enjoy himself too. He forgot about the race, about Hack and Digby waiting for Punch. He didn't even stop to think how Fred would react. The game fell into a pattern. Chase Punch, nearly catch him – Punch flies away – returns – it went on and on and on. Alfie had rarely had such fun, and exercise was so good for one!

He took no notice of express trains passing through the station, nor of the hustle and bustle when local trains arrived. But at last he lay down tired out and followed Punch's movements with his eyes. The bird flew round and round for a time and then, evidently deciding the game was finished, flew off towards the loft.

Alfie came to with a start as he watched Punch drop on to a small landing board and enter the loft through a trap door – far, far too late to win the race.

Hack still stood by the loft. Perhaps it was just as well that the railway cat couldn't see the expression on the Leading Railman's face! Alfie made his way down to the platform where Fred was dealing with some parcels.

'Well, well, well,' he said. 'Turned up at last, have you? I wonder what mischief you've been up to.'

'Miaow!' said Alfie as he rubbed his nose against Fred's shoe.

'Hm-mmm . . . You look far too innocent to be true,' said Fred.

At that moment Hack came towards them. Alfie decided against running away, but he stayed as close to Fred as possible. Fred took one look at Hack's face and raised his eyebrows. 'Didn't Punch win the race after all?' he asked.

'He did not,' replied Hack grimly. 'And all because of Alfie.'

'Because of *Alfie*? Nonsense!' cried Fred.

'It's true. I caught sight of them – too late – on the staff room roof, and it's my guess that cat was preventing Punch from flying home.'

Preventing – Alfie could hardly believe his ears. After all his efforts to chase the stupid bird off the roof! He turned his head and licked the fur on his back.

'Really, Hack, I don't believe . . .' began Fred.

He looked thoughtful. 'Er – I did notice Alfie on the roof, but there was no sign of Punch.'

'You wouldn't be able to see him from the platform,' retorted Hack. 'I'll prove to you that Punch was there. Wait!'

He strode off down the platform and returned with a ladder. He quickly climbed up on to the roof, where he disappeared from view. Soon his head appeared over the guttering.

'Watch!' he called out. He held out one hand, opened it, and down floated a few feathers. 'Punch's feathers!'

'Well, er . . . er – I see what you mean,' said Fred.

Fortunately just then, a train drew up at the platform.

'Back to business,' called Fred, with relief. 'Come down, Hack. You're on duty now.'

Alfie made himself especially pleasant to the passengers, doing his best to greet each one individually. In return he received nods, smiles and an occasional stroke or pat.

After the train had left, Hack said stubbornly,

'You *must* admit, Fred – Punch lost because of Alfie.'

'But Alfie always plays games chasing your pigeons away,' said Fred.

'Games! Huh!' cried Hack. 'Well, he's just had a very expensive game. And if he doesn't keep well away from my birds in future, I'll . . . I'll . . .'

'Oh, come now, Hack,' said Fred. 'I'm sure Alfie didn't mean any harm, even if it was his fault – which I doubt.'

'Miaow!' said Alfie. Good old Fred!

'I'm sorry Punch didn't win,' Fred went on, 'but, never mind, Hack, perhaps *Digby* will make up for it. I hear you've entered him for the Dog Championship at the County Show.'

Hack nodded. 'I'm sure Digby has a chance of winning the Cup this year,' he said more cheerfully. 'So long as that cat keeps his nose out of my affairs.'

Fred laughed. 'Alfie couldn't possibly do anything to prevent Digby winning,' he said.

'Wouldn't trust him,' muttered Hack, with a sidelong glance at Alfie, who growled just a little in his throat. 'As a matter of fact,' Hack went on, 'I've been thinking . . .'

'Miaow!' interrupted Alfie (rather rudely)!

' . . . it would be much better if we kept a dog, instead of a cat, on the station.'

'A *dog*,' cried Fred, astonished. 'What on earth would we want with a dog when we've got Alfie?'

'Well, for a start, dogs are more intelligent than cats . . .' began Hack.

'Brr-r . . . brr-r . . . brr-r . . .' grumbled Alfie. He didn't like the sound of this.

' . . . take Digby, for example.'

Digby, thought Alfie. That floppy-eared creature intelligent? Good for a lark now and then was Digby, and affectionate – but intelligent? Alfie shook his head.

'Digby?' repeated Fred. 'Huh! Give me Alfie any time.' He stroked Alfie from the top of his head down to the end of his tail. 'Make no mistake, Hack, there will be no Digby – or any other dog – on this station. And, what's more, I'd like to see Digby do anything Alfie can't do.'

'Cats!' muttered Hack, with a shrug, as he went off over the bridge.

Fred laughed out loud and Alfie rolled on to his

back. He couldn't imagine how Digby would manage to keep rats and mice away from the station. Nor how he would have the patience to see trains in and out and be friendly to the passengers all the time. There was much more to being the railway cat than one would think.

'Do try and behave yourself, Alfie,' said Fred as he went into his office and closed the door. The door reopened and Fred's head appeared. His eyes twinkled. 'But, don't worry,' he said. 'I wouldn't change you for all the Digbys in the world!' Fred's head disappeared and the door closed again.

Alfie walked out of the station with his head and tail held high. Trust Fred to stick up for him. Still, Alfie felt just a little bit guilty. Had he tried hard enough to send Punch home in time to win the race?

He sat down outside the station. While he kept his eyes and ears open for anything interesting, he wondered how he could please Hack by helping Digby to win the Cup.

He *must* think of a way.

He strolled down the road and stopped outside Hack's garden gate. Digby soon scented Alfie and

dashed round from the back of the house. The dog yelped and barked loudly as he jumped up and down against the gate in his efforts to get at Alfie.

Alfie felt very superior as he sat and stared at Digby through the bars. He, Alfie, might be only a cat (according to Hack!) but he was never fenced in like Digby. Fancy being unable to take a walk whenever one felt like it, even at midnight – or retire into a corner of the station when one wanted to be quiet.

Alfie wouldn't choose a cooped-up dog's life for anything. But, back to the question in mind. How was he going to help Digby to win the Cup?

Leaving the dog to his now frenzied barking, Alfie, deep in thought, returned to his station duties. He'd start watching right away for an opportunity to help Digby.

He hadn't long to wait.

3

The Obedience Class

The very next Saturday morning when Alfie was sunning himself outside the station Hack, who was off duty, came down the road with Digby on a lead.

Odd, thought Alfie. Hack and Digby usually went the other way up to the five-acre field for a walk and a romp – not often enough, though thought Alfie.

Fred appeared. ' 'Morning, Hack,' he called. 'Taking Digby shopping?'

'Er, yes – well, no,' said Hack. 'As a matter of fact we're going to the obedience class in the village hall.'

'*Obedience* class!' exclaimed Fred. 'For you or for Digby?'

'*Dog* obedience class,' said Hack, glaring at Fred. 'Not that Digby needs instruction,' he added hastily. 'He's just going along for a refresher course – to keep him in trim for the Show.'

Fred raised his eyebrows. Hack jerked the lead as Digby edged towards Alfie. 'Come on, Digby,' he said. Off they went with Digby straining at the lead.

'I'd like to be in the hall this morning,' said Fred with a grin.

'Miaow!' agreed Alfie. He'd already decided to go along to the hall – might learn something useful. Alfie always preferred to please himself what he did, but he wasn't going to miss an opportunity of watching Digby in training and, if possible, finding a way of helping him.

Alfie made his way through back gardens and over fences to the hall, where he jumped up on to a sill and gazed through a window. The dog trainer was arranging chairs in a wide circle. The man left the hall and, quick as a flash, Alfie was through the partly-open window. Then, with a couple of leaps and a scramble, he reached a high shelf. He lay down behind two piles of books, from where he had a very good view of the hall through a gap between the books.

The trainer returned and gradually the hall

began to fill with owners and dogs.

'Take a seat everyone,' called the trainer.

Alfie kept a sharp look-out for Digby. Ah, yes, there he was, pulling so hard on the lead that Hack fairly shot through the doorway into the hall.

Soon every seat was occupied by a dog owner. Alfie counted at least seven different breeds of dogs. He recognised the butcher's long-haired hound and old Mrs Taylor's dumpy Pekinese and a few others – and, of course, Digby.

There was a great deal of yapping and barking, even whining (to Alfie's disgust) from some of the dogs until the trainer put up a hand.

'Quiet, please – quiet,' he cried. Gradually there was a hush as owners managed to control their pets.

'Now we'll begin . . .' said the man.

But just then Digby looked up at the shelf and started howling. He jumped about and pulled a red-faced Hack right off his chair.

Digby *knows* I'm here – now that shows intelligence, thought Alfie.

'Please restrain your dog, Mr Hack,' said the trainer.

Hack did his best and the instruction began. A small dog and its owner went into the middle of the ring. The trainer held the lead. 'Walk!' he ordered. The dog looked up at him, got the message, walked alongside the man, and after that obeyed nearly every command.

Very good, thought Alfie. He hoped Digby would do as well. Each dog had a turn. Some were quick to learn, others had to be coaxed and told what to do over and over again.

Really, thought Alfie! Fred had only to tell him anything *once* and he understood what was required. How much more intelligent cats were than dogs.

Digby was very uneasy as he awaited his turn. He constantly glanced up at the shelf and occasionally gave a short, sharp bark. Once he sprang up and pulled on the lead.

'Down, Digby – *down!*' hissed Hack as he pushed the dog flat on the floor.

Poor Digby, how undignified, thought Alfie.

And then it was Digby's turn. Hack led him into the ring. Alfie felt very excited. He must watch

carefully. He leaned forward and – to his horror! –
a pile of books slid off the shelf and fell to the floor
with a crash. Alfie found himself in full view of
everyone. In a panic, he took a flying leap off the
shelf and fled into a corner.

'It's Alfie!' yelled Hack, exasperated, whereupon
Digby pulled him right off his feet and dragged him
along the floor.

'Oh! Ow! Ouch!' shouted Hack as his elbow hit
the floor. Pandemonium broke out as all the dogs
started barking. Digby managed to reach Alfie,
who boxed him across the nose. The dog drew
back, but unexpectedly launched another attack.
Taken by surprise, Alfie scratched Digby's nose.

Oh – I didn't *mean* to do that, he thought guil-
tily.

The trainer grabbed Alfie and held him in his
arms. He waited while Digby had a plaster put on
his nose then, still holding Alfie, he addressed the
class.

'Dogs must be trained to get used to cats, to treat
them with respect,' he said, with a long stare at the
unfortunate Hack.

'Miaow!' said Alfie, very pleased with this statement.

The man looked down at him. 'And there's no need for you to be afraid of dogs, Alfie,' he said.

'Miaow?' said Alfie again. Afraid of dogs? Me? Not likely. He rubbed his head under the man's chin.

'You'd better sit down quietly somewhere until we've finished,' said the man.

Alfie jumped down and sat upright by the trainer, with his front paws side by side. He looked up at the man as if to ask, What about *my* training?

The trainer looked surprised. 'I'll guarantee this cat could show your dogs a thing or two,' he said to the class. 'Come on, Alfie – walk!'

Always willing to oblige, thought Alfie, as he trotted beside the man all the way down the long hall and back again.

'Stay!' was the next order, as the trainer put out a hand and went off down the hall on his own.

That's easy, thought Alfie. He stayed.

'Come!' was the next command and, waving the tip of his tail, Alfie galloped towards him. This *was* a good game, almost as enjoyable as the one he'd had with Punch. He must encourage Fred to join in.

'Good cat. *Good* cat!' said the trainer. 'He's an example to all. Now we'll have the next dog, please.'

Alfie sat down in the corner again and watched Digby put through his paces. Digby didn't show to advantage. He went plod-plod-plod down the hall instead of walking briskly, and he refused to come when called.

Suddenly Alfie had an inspiration. He *knew* now what was wrong with Digby. The dog was out of condition. He needed far more exercise than Hack gave him. Now Alfie realised how he could help Digby to win the Cup – get him to take more exercise. Alfie was determined that somehow – he didn't yet know *how* – he would see that Digby was encouraged to run and run – and run!

Soon the class was dismissed and dogs and owners left the hall. Alfie followed at a safe distance behind Hack and Digby. Fred was outside the station. Alfie rushed up and weaved in and out of

Fred's legs. 'Prrr-rr . . . Prrr-rr . . . Prrr-rr . . .' he sang.

As Hack and Digby came up Fred called out, 'Had a good morning, Hack – Digby do well?'

Hack didn't answer and then Fred noticed the plaster on Digby's nose. 'Oh, dear,' he said. 'What-ever . . .?'

'That cat can't keep his claws to himself,' burst out Hack.

'That's not true,' said Fred firmly. 'Alfie *never* uses his claws unless he's provoked.'

'Miaow!' said Alfie. In any case, it was only a surface scratch – hardly drew blood. It would heal long before the Show.

Digby broke loose and, with his mouth wide open, rushed up to Alfie. He stopped short within an inch or two of Alfie's nose. What good sharp teeth he's got, thought Alfie admiringly. They'll help to win him marks at the Show. He sat and stared at Digby without blinking once.

Fred came to the rescue. 'Now then, you two,' he said. 'You'll have to learn to live peaceably as neighbours.'

'Miaow!' But we *do* – why can't they understand?

'Woof! Woof! Woof!' agreed Digby.

'Alfie couldn't live peaceably with anyone,' cried Hack.

'Nonsense! I agree Alfie can be, well, er . . . mischievous at times,' said Fred. 'But he's still the most friendly and intelligent cat on the whole railway system.'

'You don't know what you're talking about,' said Hack. 'Come on, Digby.' Off they went home.

When they were out of sight Fred wagged a finger at Alfie. 'Really, Alfie!' he said. 'Digby can be an excellent dog, you know. He could be very intelligent if he tried a bit harder – and if Hack didn't give in to him so much *and* – most important – if he had more exercise.'

'Miaow!' said Alfie. Digby *was* going to have much more exercise, come what may.

'Keep out of Digby's way until after the Show,' ordered Fred.

Keep out of Digby's way? That was the very last thing Alfie intended. He'd got to work hard on

Digby to get some of the fat off him.

'Saucer of milk, Alfie?' said Fred.

'Miaow!' Please!

They went into the staff room together. Fred stayed and had a cup of tea while Alfie drank the milk. Life could be very pleasant when one had an understanding friend like Fred around, thought the railway cat.

The Chase

It was only two weeks to the County Show. I *must* get busy with Digby right away, thought Alfie. Next day, when Hack was on duty, he noticed Mrs Hack, with a basket over one arm, going past the station on her way to the village. It had been raining but the sky had cleared and the sun was peeping through the clouds. There was a good chance that Digby would have been given the run of the garden.

Off ran the railway cat up the road. He jumped up on to the high wall enclosing Hack's garden, where he stopped short in surprise. Hack had lined the top of the wall with barbed-wire entanglements – to keep out cats, including Alfie!

What a lark, he thought, as he carefully stepped over the wire from one end of the wall to the other, without as much as scratching a toe nail. He'd show Hack what cats were made of!

He could see Digby stretched out by the kitchen

door, watching him. Punch and the other pigeons were asleep in their loft against the far wall. Alfie leapt on to a convenient tree branch overhanging the garden and sat down. Digby got up and rushed across the lawn. He stood on his hind legs scratching at the tree trunk with blunt claws, while Alfie sat calmly on the branch above his head. What a good thing dogs were unable to climb trees, thought Alfie.

He got up, yawned and stretched himself. Just then another cat appeared on the wall. Digby turned his head and, quick as lightning, Alfie slid down the trunk and landed in the garden – in Digby's own territory. He ran. After him came Digby. Round and round they sped, through the flower beds and the vegetable patch, across the lawn, round to the front of the house and back again, churning up mud as they went.

They had a strenuous time, stopping only now and then for a brief rest. What excellent exercise Digby was having, thought Alfie. If they could only do this every day until the Show, the dog would be as fit as a fiddle.

Alfie pricked up his ears as the garden gate clicked. Mrs Hack had returned. Time to go. Back at the station he slipped into the staff room and curled up in a chair. It was hard work getting Digby into condition, he thought, as he closed his eyes.

Hack came in. 'Huh! Tired out so early in the day?' he remarked. 'Up to no good, I suppose – as usual.'

'Miaow!' said Alfie indignantly, without opening his eyes. *You'll* never guess what I've been doing for Digby.

But Hack guessed as soon as he saw the condition of his garden. Flowers and vegetables uprooted, grass flattened and mud everywhere. He dashed back to the station and ran into the staff room to see Fred. Alfie slept on.

'That cat's been in my garden tantalising Digby,' he stormed. 'I'll keep him out. You'll see. I'll teach him a lesson . . . I'll . . .'

There's no peace, sighed Alfie, as he opened one eye to look at Hack. Really, the man was beside himself. What a fuss about damage to a garden when there were far more important matters to be

considered – Show Day, for instance.

When Hack, muttering to himself, had left, Fred picked Alfie up and put him on a table. 'No use struggling,' he said firmly. All Alfie wanted just then was sleep, and more sleep.

'Um . . . just look at the state of your fur. *Alfie*, you disobedient cat – you *have* been in Hack's garden!'

'Miaow!' agreed Alfie. And you'd thank me if you knew why I've been there.

'Well, I'm going to give you a thorough clean-up,' said Fred. 'And make sure you stay clean. You've got to be in good trim for . . . never mind what.'

'Miaow?' said Alfie, puzzled. Never mind *what*?

Fred opened a cupboard, took out a brush and comb and began to groom Alfie. He brushed and combed until the railway cat felt that every hair on his body and every whisker on his face had been dealt with. My word, Fred had really got a bee in his bonnet about cleanliness. This must be what was meant by spring cleaning! Or perhaps the Area Manager was due to inspect the station?

Fred finished at last. He pulled Alfie's ears gently. 'See you stay away from Hack's garden – or I'll lock you in the staff room,' he threatened.

But nothing was going to stop Alfie from visiting Digby. He never missed a single opportunity of dropping into the garden and allowing Digby to chase him. Once or twice Hack caught them at it. Each time he shouted and shook his fist as Alfie made a hasty retreat. But Alfie returned time after time. Fred tried locking him up, but he always managed to escape.

But the railway cat was worried. Digby was certainly thinner – well he might be! – but in Alfie's opinion the dog still panted too much. His lungs had not yet had enough exercise. It was now Thursday, only two more days to the Show.

Alfie thought about the matter all day. During that night when he was patrolling the station, he heard a loud clanging noise outside. The station dustbin lid! He stood still, with ears raised and one paw held high. There wasn't any wind so who, or what, had knocked off the lid? Then there was a scuffling sound.

Cats, guessed Alfie. Greedy, overfed domestic cats with nothing better to do than raid dustbins for odd scraps of food they didn't need. He'd see them off!

He made his way out of the station. To his surprise there wasn't a cat in sight but, clearly visible in the moonlight, was Digby fighting a large rat for possession of the dustbin. (However had Digby managed to get out of the house, wondered Alfie?)

Alfie settled down in a corner and watched. Should he join in the fray? Then a better idea struck him. Here was a golden opportunity, perhaps the last, to get Digby on the run. He crept up stealthily behind Digby and let out an ear-splitting, 'MIAOW-MIAOW-MIAOW ... AOW ... AOW ...'

Digby jumped and turned round. Alfie spat at him, then dashed off down the village street. Digby abandoned the dustbin to the rat and raced after him. Down the street they ran, turned left and followed a bridle path as far as the gravel pit. Round and round – and round! – the pit they sped, then

back to the road and right through some roadworks
and sticky tar into the main street again.

Alfie was beginning to feel exhausted. Now *he*
was panting! He glanced back to see Digby, looking
quite fierce, still pounding after him. Oh, dear!
Alfie hoped his friend realised this was for his own
good – and supposed to be fun as well.

But Digby was gaining ground – he was far too
close for comfort. As they went past the church
Alfie remembered having noticed the steeplejack at
work high up on the church spire during the day.
He swerved and, managing to evade Digby,
jumped the gate leading into the churchyard. To
his relief he saw the steeplejack's ladders still in
position. He took a flying leap on to the bottom
rung of a ladder and quickly made his way upwards
until he reached a second ladder, which led him
right to the top of the spire.

Behind him Digby scrambled on to the first
ladder, but his weight pulled it from its moorings
and it crashed to the ground. From his high perch
Alfie watched as Digby, tail between his legs, ran
off homewards.

51

To Alfie the ground seemed a long way off. However was he going to get down? Carefully he stretched out on the ledge below the weathercock. He was thankful it was a calm, clear night. A wind at this moment would be his worst enemy.

If he hadn't felt so insecure he would have admired the view all round. Hearing a familiar sound he raised his head, and soon a train – the late-night express from Bristol – rushed under the road bridge and through the station on its way to London. How Alfie wished he was on the train instead of being stranded on top of the church spire.

He started when he heard a faint noise far below. He looked down. To his amazement he saw two white-clad figures emerge from the church. Alfie's fur stood on end and he trembled with fright. Ghosts! No doubt about that. What other white figures would be coming out of a church at nearly midnight?

Alfie feared the ghosts would catch sight of him, float to the top of the spire and . . . and . . . and . . . he couldn't bear to imagine what might happen to him. He moved nervously and nearly fell off the ledge.

'*Miaow*!' he moaned.

The two figures looked up.

'It's a cat!' exclaimed one ghost.

'It's no ordinary cat – it's our Alfie,' shouted the other ghost.

Not the other ghost, for Alfie had immediately recognised *Hack's* voice. He sighed with relief – but whatever was the stupid man doing at midnight looking like a ghost? Anyhow, it explained why Digby was out at night on his own. The dog must have escaped from the house to follow his master.

Hack went on shouting, 'I give up my sleep to do a voluntary rushed job to decorate the church in time for the festival and what do I find? Alfie up to mischief again!'

'Well, it's no use grumbling. We'll have to get him down somehow,' said the other man. 'What about sending for the steeplejack?'

'That would take far too long – he lives about ten miles away. Much better to send for the fire brigade. I'll go and rouse the vicar and use his phone.

You open the gate for the brigade.'

Off went a much displeased Hack. He returned with the vicar and very soon a siren was heard in the distance and the fire engine arrived. It turned into the churchyard and drew up at the church door. By this time several villagers, disturbed by the commotion, had arrived on the scene.

The firemen jumped down and immediately began to uncoil the hoses. 'Where's the fire?' one shouted.

'There's no fire,' cried Hack. 'It's Alfie, up there.' He pointed.

'Alfie? Alfie who? Oh, you mean *Alfie*, the railway cat. That won't do. Trains wouldn't run without him on duty. We'll soon have him down.'

He looked up at the spire. 'We'll use the aerial ladder,' he decided.

Alfie watched as the ladder emerged from a chassis on the engine and started to rise, up and up and up until it stopped right in front of him. Swiftly the fireman climbed up to the top of the ladder and grabbed Alfie.

'Miaow . . . aow . . . aow . . .!' cried Alfie as he

snuggled up against the man's jacket for the downward trip.

Everyone, except Hack, clustered round to make sure the railway cat was uninjured, but Hack called out, 'Get back to the station, Alfie, and look for mice – that's your job, not climbing church steeples.'

'Brrr . . . rrr . . . rrr . . .' growled Alfie. Silly man. He thinks I climbed up there on purpose, does he? Nevertheless, to avoid further trouble, Alfie strolled back to the station.

Next morning Fred came along to the staff room. 'I've heard all about your little escapade, Alfie,' he cried. 'Let me have a look at you.'

Oh, no, not *another* grooming, groaned Alfie to himself. Whatever was the matter with Fred – his best friend – always wanting to clean him up, day after day after day. Surely spring cleaning didn't go on for ever?

But Fred was determined. He brushed and combed Alfie and, noticing one or two specks of tar on his fur, produced some cleaning fluid and rubbed and rubbed until there wasn't a trace of the sticky stuff left.

The Chase

As soon as Fred had finished with him Alfie, in high spirits, ran out and rolled over and over in the loose soil on one of the rose beds. Fred came out and shook his fist at him – which surprised Alfie very much. Fred had never done that before.

However, Alfie felt happy. Digby had had lots of exercise last night. There could be no doubt now about him bringing home the Cup on Saturday.

5

Show Day

On Friday night Alfie went to bed far too excited to sleep for thinking about Digby. Next morning he was up long before the London overnight express had passed through the station. For something to do he sat down on the platform and licked himself all over – not that it was necessary after all Fred's efforts to keep him clean!

The express went through the station with a whoosh! and a roar! Alfie made his way to the gate. He knew that Hack had taken a day's leave to go with Digby to the Show. Fred would see to breakfast, thought Alfie, but to his surprise a reliefman was the first to report for duty.

'Miaow?' Alfie said. Where's Fred?

'Ready for breakfast, old chap?' asked the man. 'Well, Fred won't be coming on duty until the evening shift, but don't worry, Brown will soon be here.'

Brown arrived and Alfie hadn't long to wait for his meal. Afterwards he hurried back over the bridge to the Down platform, from where he had no intention of moving until he had watched Digby's departure by the 9.30 local train – a fitter, leaner Digby thanks to his friend, the railway cat! And Alfie also intended being on the Up platform to greet Digby on his return with the silver Cup. It promised to be an exciting day.

Five minutes or so before the train was due Fred, dressed for an outing and carrying a large covered basket, came on to the platform.

He's going fishing, guessed Alfie. Do him good. In Alfie's opinion Fred had been working too hard lately. He rolled over and over at Fred's feet.

'Hey there – stop that, Alfie, you'll get dusty!' cried Fred as he bent down and flapped a large handkerchief over Alfie's back, sides and stomach. Alfie enjoyed this but, really, Fred *was* overdoing things.

Digby burst on to the platform pulling Hack after him. Alfie purred with pleasure at the sight of this alert, bright-eyed, slim dog with the glossy coat. Fred bent down to stroke Digby.

'Best of luck, Digby,' he said.

'Woof! Woof! Woof!' barked Digby. He pulled Hack further down the platform – to keep away from Alfie and further trouble? Fred stayed with Alfie and chatted to one or two waiting passengers.

The train was announced and soon drew up at the platform. Doors opened, passengers alighted and Fred stood back to allow others to join the train. Alfie looked up at him. 'Miaow?' he said. Thought you were going fishing?

Just before the train was ready to move off, Fred bent down, lifted Alfie, put him in the basket and closed the lid. Then, holding the basket in front of him, he got into the train.

Alfie was furious. He'd been catnapped once and Fred knew how he hated being shut up anywhere. The railway cat's wailing became louder and louder.

'Shush! Shush!' said Fred as he opened the basket lid and stroked Alfie.

'Miao . . . aow . . . aow . . .' grumbled Alfie. But, after protesting for a good ten minutes he

decided to make the best of things. After all, Fred had never let him down yet. He closed his eyes.

'That's better, Alfie,' said Fred soothingly.

It was only a short journey to the town. When the train stopped Fred shut the lid, got off the train and started walking. Alfie enjoyed the slight swinging sensation in time to Fred's footsteps. Soon he could tell that Fred was walking on grass, and he could hear people shouting, and music in the background. Through a slit in the side of the basket Alfie caught sight of a large white tent.

Then it dawned on him! They were on the Show ground! Alfie felt excited. How kind of Fred. He must be taking him, Alfie, the railway cat, to see his friend Digby win the Silver Cup. Now he understood everything; why Fred looked so smart; why he had groomed Alfie to make sure the railway cat looked presentable for his outing. Alfie was sure Fred would let him out of the basket and hold him up to watch Digby in the competition.

But Alfie was wrong. They entered a large marquee. Fred put down the basket, opened the lid and popped Alfie into a small cage, with a metal floor and top and sides of wire. He, Alfie, cooped up in a *cage*! Fred must have gone right out of his mind.

But Fred was smiling as he closed the cage door. 'Now Alfie, just settle down. I'll be near at hand when the judging takes place.'

You could have knocked Alfie down with a feather. Judging what? There wasn't a dog to be seen, although Alfie could distinguish sounds of yapping and barking not far distant. But numbered cages, each with a cat inside, formed a ring round the tent.

Alfie glanced round. All sorts of cats! In one section long-haired cats, in another short-haired cats, in yet another he recognised blue-eyed, sleek-coated Siamese cats – in fact, all breeds of cats, including a group of ordinary-looking cats like Alfie himself.

How could Fred be so foolish as to think of entering Alfie in such a contest? Why, he wouldn't stand a chance against some of these beauties. He, Alfie, was a *railway* cat, not a show cat! He began to worry about Fred.

But Fred said, 'You're No.14 in the Working Cats section, Alfie, so do your best for the railway.'

Working cats! Well, that was quite a different kettle of fish, thought Alfie. The show manager's voice came over the loud speakers,

'Will all exhibitors leave the tent, please. Judging will now commence.'

'Good luck, Alfie,' said Fred. He waved as he followed other owners out of the tent.

The Siamese cats were first to be judged. Each cat in turn was taken out of its cage and put on the judge's table for examination. It was some time before it was Alfie's turn. He sat very still and quiet during the inspection of teeth, ears, face, paws, nails, whiskers – would the man never finish?

'Miaow!' he said once. I might not be a *pretty* cat, but I know I could win a prize as best mouser or best ratter!

When the judge had finished he whispered into Alfie's left ear, 'Very good, Alfie – extremely well-behaved.'

'Miaow!' said Alfie again. I'm always well-behaved – or nearly always.

Alfie was returned to the cage. By now he was enjoying himself. It was fun being with the other cats with Fred not far away. Several times he wondered how Digby was getting on and whether he, Alfie, would be given a fish supper to celebrate Digby's winning the Cup?

When the last cat had been dealt with, the owners were allowed to return to the tent. Soon the manager's voice was heard again. Starting with the Siamese, he called out the winners in each section. When he came to Working Cats, Fred stood very still, hands in pockets, while Alfie pricked up his ears.

'Winner of the Working Cats section – No.14. Alfie, the railway cat,' came the announcement.

People clapped and cheered. Fred threw up his arms and waved them about excitedly. 'What do you think of that, Alfie?' he cried. 'You've won a certificate.'

A certificate, thought Alfie. What do I want with that? A whole salmon – or half a salmon – would be more appropriate.

'Now we come to the best *overall* winner – Best Cat in the Show,' the voice continued. There was a pause and Fred shuffled his feet. 'Best Cat in the

Show – No.14 Alfie, the railway cat.'

This time Fred was speechless for at least half a minute. Then he burst out, 'You've won a prize, Alfie – a real silver Cup!'

'Miaow!' said Alfie. What did he want with a *Cup*? He wouldn't be able to get his head inside such an object.

He sat on the judge's table again while Fred received the award. Amid laughter, Fred produced a small bottle of milk and filled the Cup. He placed it in front of Alfie, who put his nose in, stuck out his tongue and lapped loudly. Cream! But, to his disgust, as he had thought, he could only reach the top of the cream.

'Never mind, Alfie,' said Fred. 'You can finish it off back at the station.'

That suited Alfie – but fancy winning a useless thing like a silver Cup! He hoped Digby's Cup would be much, much larger! As Fred had to be back on duty by evening, he and Alfie left the Show before they had time to find out how Digby was getting on.

At the station everyone congratulated the railway

cat on winning the Cup, which was placed in a locked glass-fronted case on a shelf in the booking office, for all to admire.

While Fred went about his duties, Alfie lay curled up on a station bench to await the arrival of Digby with his trophy. Nothing disturbed the railway cat for the next hour – not the coming and going of passengers, nor the arrival and departure of trains, but he opened his eyes when Digby's train was due.

Alfie jumped down as Fred came along to meet the in-coming train – with Digby and the Cup aboard! As the passengers left the train, Alfie's head jerked from left to right and from right to left, but there was no sign of the dog. Last but one to alight was Hack, then came Digby.

Digby looked happy enough and when he saw Alfie he lunged forward and jerked the lead out of Hack's hand. Alfie retreated behind Fred. 'Woof! Woof! Woof!' barked Digby as he wagged his tail.

Fred called out, 'Where's the Cup, Hack?'

'No Cup,' said Hack, gloomily. 'Lost a few vital marks for spots of tar on his coat. *Tar* – where did he get that from, I wonder?' He gave Alfie a suspicious glance.

Fred also stared at Alfie, as he eased his cap from his forehead, but all he said was, 'Well, that's a pity, but never mind, Hack, there's another Show in two months' time. Digby is in such good condition I'm sure he's worthy of winning any competition.'

Hack sighed and nodded. Off he went with Digby. Alfie felt very upset. *He* hadn't wanted to win a Cup – Fred shouldn't have entered him in the Show. He stared at his friend reproachfully, then jumped on to the bench, lay down and closed his eyes.

'Don't worry, Alfie,' said Fred. 'That's how it is – but *tar*, now I wonder . . .?'

Alfie opened one eye.

'. . . and don't look at me with that butter-wouldn't-melt-in-your-mouth expression!'

Alfie got up, turned his back on Fred and lay down again. It was very difficult trying to do the right thing all the time, he thought.

He was soon fast asleep.

6

The Bullion Bag

That night Alfie decided he was in need of fresh air and exercise, so he started off along the top of the railway embankment. At a point not far from the station a lane, bordered by a strong wire fence, ran alongside the railway track for a short distance.

Alfie sat down to wait for the east-bound night parcels train to pass. There was a full moon. The driver would probably see him and wave. He turned his head as he heard a faint sound. A van, without lights, was being driven very slowly along the lane. Alfie lay down flat as the vehicle came to a standstill opposite him. He noticed that the van carried no trade name or other identification. He overheard two men talking.

'Just our luck – it must be running late,' said one man.

'Well, we daren't risk standing here,' said the other man. 'Drive back to the hide-out. We'll wait there ten minutes before returning. It should have passed by then.'

The van did a three-point turn and moved off. Now what could be running late but a train – the parcels train perhaps – thought Alfie? But why were these men so interested in a train?

He resumed his waiting position, but soon another car approached. Goodness, why such activity in the middle of the night? It was getting almost like Piccadilly Circus! This time it was a Panda car with side lights showing. Alfie was always happy to see his friends the police, so he climbed up the wire fence and balanced on top of one of the concrete support posts. He miaowed loudly.

'Why, hello, Alfie,' called the constable cheerfully. 'You on duty, too?'

The sergeant beside him leaned forward. 'Well, let us know if you see or hear anything suspicious,' he called out.

The car moved off slowly.

Hmmm . . . mmm . . . I *could* have told them about the unmarked van, thought Alfie. Soon he heard the parcels train in the distance. As it drew level the driver leaned out of the engine cab and waved to Alfie.

As the guard's van passed, something came flying out of the van window. Alfie ducked and fell off the post. A large bag, which had just missed his head, burst open as it hit the ground. Alfie's eyes widened at the sight of hundreds and hundreds – perhaps *thousands* – of coins, glinting in the moonlight, strewn over the grass.

Could they possibly be *gold* coins? If so, what a lot of fish and cream could be bought with all that money. But what did it all mean, thought Alfie? An unmarked van with no lights – a police car obviously on the alert – money thrown out of a train – was there a connection?

Alfie looked up to see the van coming back. His mind worked quickly. These men must be in league with whoever had thrown the bag out of the train and had come to collect the haul.

But it would take them much longer to pick up the money than they had expected. No doubt they had planned to snatch the bag and be off at full speed. They were going to have a shock.

Alfie decided this was no place for him at the moment. The men might be armed. How could he raise the alarm? Hastily he jumped the fence and streaked off down the lane in the direction of the station. As he passed Hack's house, Digby started to bark.

Alfie stopped short, turned and squeezed under the gate. He sprang on to the kitchen window sill and clawed at the glass with his front paws. Inside, Digby howled and yelped as he jumped on to the sink and tried to get at Alfie through the glass.

Digby made such a commotion that Hack came stumbling down the stairs and probably thinking there must be an intruder outside, opened the kitchen door. Out shot Digby.

And off the sill leapt Alfie, under the gate and back up the lane. He glanced back to see Digby jump right over the gate. My word, I've never seen him do that before, thought Alfie. What a fit dog he is now!

Alfie reached the van, with Digby not far behind. The two men were on the embankment frantically stuffing handfuls of gold coins into the torn bullion bag and into their pockets. Alfie skidded to a halt but Digby tore past him and, with a howl, fell on one of the men. The other man looked up horrified, ran off, got into the van and, with a grinding of gears, drove off. The robber left on the embankment struggled as a snarling Digby, with teeth bared and ears flattened, pressed him to the ground.

Digby is *magnificent* in a crisis, thought Alfie. Suddenly the man exerted all his strength to push Digby away. Alfie wasn't having that. He scrambled down the slope and with claws unsheathed, crashed on top of the man while Digby managed to regain his hold by sinking his teeth into the man's sweater.

'Two of them! Help! Help!' screamed the man, as he fought to get free.

Alfie was beginning to think they wouldn't be able to restrain the man much longer when he looked up to see his two policemen friends dashing to the rescue. He jumped off the robber and ran behind a tree. Digby couldn't be persuaded to let go of his victim. But soon a breathless Hack arrived

and pulled his dog away.

As handcuffs were clapped on to the criminal's wrists, the sergeant said, 'At least we've caught one of the gang, thanks to your S.O.S., Mr Hack.'

'And thanks also to Digby,' put in the constable. 'You'd both better come along to the police station with us.'

'Here come the reinforcements,' cried the sergeant as another police car drove up.

Alfie watched as Hack and Digby joined the two policemen and the criminal in the first car. It drove off down the lane, leaving the others to guard the bullion.

Alfie went back to the station. As it was such a fine night he settled down on a bench and was soon fast asleep.

He was still there when Fred woke him next morning.

'Come on, lazy bones, breakfast's ready,' cried Fred as he gave the railway cat a playful push.

'Miaow!' said Alfie, as he stretched himself and yawned. Lazy, indeed! *You* don't know what I was up to last night. In the staff room, Alfie listened to

Fred and Hack talking about the night's events.

'The criminals hid in the guard's van before the train started, overpowered the guard, tied him up and then threw out the bullion at the appointed place. They escaped from the train when it slowed down at a signal.'

'Well, I hear they've all been rounded up,' said Fred, 'and Digby must be given credit for making the first capture.'

Hack nodded. Then he glanced at Alfie. 'Alfie was there as well. I caught sight of him behind a tree,' he said.

'Not surprised to hear that Alfie had a paw in it,' said Fred, laughing. 'But it was definitely Digby's night, and I reckon he deserves at least a silver Cup, don't you, Alfie?'

'Miaow!' said Alfie. Certainly he does.

Life at the station went on normally for a time. Then one day there was great activity – much cleaning and polishing, weeding of flower beds and washing of platforms and windows. *More* spring cleaning, wondered Alfie – or a station inspection?

That evening Fred brushed and combed Alfie

vigorously, a sure sign that something out of the ordinary could be expected. Next morning Alfie was up bright and early.

'Area Manager's arriving on the 10.30, Alfie,' Fred called out as he busied himself about the station. At 10.15 Hack went home and returned with Digby. Mrs Hack came along as well, so Alfie knew this was going to be no ordinary inspection. And there were cameramen and reporters on the station.

At 10.15 everyone lined up on the platform as the train came in. Out stepped the Area Manager. Alfie had hoped the V.I.P. had arrived to present a silver Cup to Digby. But the man was carrying only a flat briefcase – and surely a *Cup* wouldn't fit into that? Alfie was *very* disappointed.

And after all Digby didn't receive a Cup. The Manager shook hands with everybody, patted Digby and stroked Alfie. Then he took a small box out of the briefcase, opened the box and held up something round, bright and shining.

'I have great pleasure,' he said, 'in presenting this pure gold medal to Digby, for Animal Bravery

in tackling and holding a dangerous criminal.'

The man bent down and fastened the medal on to Digby's collar. Cameras clicked. Digby wagged his tail and barked. Everyone clapped and Alfie miaowed.

After the brief ceremony was over and the Manager had departed, people gathered round to congratulate Digby and to examine the medal, while Mr and Mrs Hack stood by proudly.

Fred turned to Alfie. 'Everything's turned out well, eh, Alfie?' he said. 'Punch lost the race, but Digby's got a gold medal, so Hack is satisfied.' His eyes twinkled. 'A gold medal is more valuable than a silver Cup isn't it, Alfie?'

'Miaow!' Yes, Alfie supposed it was, but *he* wasn't interested in a Cup or a medal. Next year at the County Show – or the year after, or the year after that – he might try to win a silver *Saucer*. That would be valuable. After all a good-sized saucer could hold a lot of milk – or cream!

Alfie decided to get into training right away. He was never one to let the grass grow under his paws.